This book belongs to

....

....

For Celia
with thanks
L.P.

This edition first published in 2019 by Alligator Products Ltd.
Cupcake is an imprint of Alligator Products Ltd
2nd Floor, 314 Regents Park Road, London N3 2JX

Written by Leyland Perree
Illustrated by Christina Forshay

Printed in China.1539

TOAD'S ROAD CODE

cupcake

The toad wore a coat and a big smiley grin,
and a little bow tie nestled under his chin.
His home was a hole at the side of the brook.
It was neat, it was tidy. Come in, take a look!

This toad was a traveller and he liked to roam
all over the marshes surrounding his home.
But one day he thought, "I think I shall wander
to visit my cousin who lives way out yonder."

From his cosy toad hole, he skipped and he hopped
with a nice gooey cake (which he never once dropped).
He whistled a tune as he bounced and he bopped
to the road at the end of the marsh... where he stopped.

"How-diddly-do will I make it across
with neither myself nor the cake getting squashed?
But I'm due at my cousin's for afternoon tea,
so how hard can it be? I mean, seriously?"

So straightening his tie, he set off at a pace.
With a hop, skip and jump (and with admirable grace),
he launched himself into the first lane he saw
and met with a terrible ear-splitting ROAR!

"YIKES!" went the toad leaping out of his skin,
as he covered his ears at the terrible din.
Frightened, he flattened himself to the road.
"Goodness, what WAS that? Did something EXPLODE?"

No – it was only the sound of a car,
which passed him close-by and zoomed off to afar.
The toad though had been given a bit of a start,
and lay in the road with his hand on his heart.

"How-diddly-do will I ever manage
to cross the next lane without any damage?
But I'm due at my cousin's for afternoon tea,
so how hard can it be? I mean, seriously?"

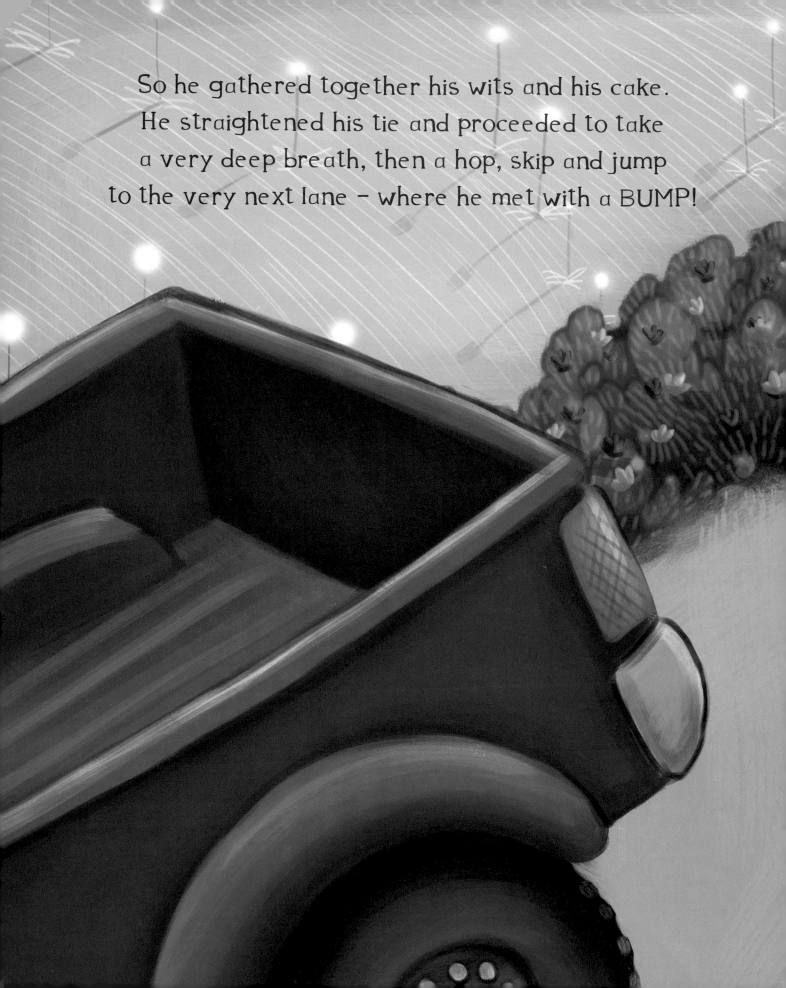

So he gathered together his wits and his cake.
He straightened his tie and proceeded to take
a very deep breath, then a hop, skip and jump
to the very next lane – where he met with a BUMP!

Up in the air went the cake and the toad.
SPLAT! went the cake as it squished on the road.
"YIKES!" went the toad, landing safe on the bank,
Startled and shaken. "What WAS that? A TANK?"

No, not a tank – just a really big truck
(which the toad was glad that he'd managed to duck).
The cake though had taken the brunt of the wallop,
and lay on the road in a big, gooey dollop.

"MY CAKE!" wailed the toad as the truck flew on by.
But he brushed himself down, then he straightened his tie.
And picking up all that remained of his cake,
carried on to his cousin's small house by the lake.

"How-do-you-diddly-do," said the toad.
"I'm so glad to see you." (And GOODNESS, it showed!)
"Come in," said his cousin. "Sit down if you're able.
We'll have us some nice, gooey cake at the table."

The toad sat with his cousin (a frog) and they nattered
of Frog-and-Toad things, and of family matters.
When finally their chat came around to the road,
and how to cross safely: the road safety code.

TOAD ROAD CODE

STOP! at the drop,
(it's too dangerous to hop!)
LOOK! for things wheeled,
(better keep your eyes peeled!)
LISTEN! all around,
(can you hear any sound?)
If there's nothing that you
can see or can hear,
then hop right across –
you have nothing to fear!

The toad thanked his cousin, and ate some more cake,
and finally looked at his watch – it was late.
"Well, thanks for tip (and the cake and the tea),
but I'd better be going now. Seriously."

The frog gave him a hug, then gave the toad his jacket
and the last piece of cake in a brown paper packet.
"Remember the code!" he said with a wave,
as homeward the toad hopped feeling happy and brave.

Soon, sure enough, the toad came to the place
where cars and big trucks (and more dangerous things) raced.
So he tried to remember his cousin's advice.
"Here goes," said the toad – and he reminded himself twice.

"STOP! LOOK! and LISTEN!" the toad's cousin had said.
So, mopping droplets of sweat from his head,
he stopped at the kerb, cupped his ear and then watched,
and when all was clear, he hopped safely across.

"HOORAY!" laughed the toad in delight (and relief).
Then he stuck out his chin, with that tie underneath,
which he straightened once more so it didn't look funny
and bounced all the way home – just as brisk as a bunny.

"How-diddly-HAPPY I am to be back!"
Said the toad as he hung up his coat on the rack.
He loosened his tie and he said (loudly yawning),
"I think I shall visit again in the morning."

The toad wore a coat and a big toothy grin,
And a little bow tie nestled under his chin.
He lives in a brook by a marsh near a road,
which he crosses quite often –
all thanks to the CODE.

"Can you remember the CODE?"

TOAD ROAD CODE

STOP! at the drop,
(it's too dangerous to hop!)
LOOK! for things wheeled,
(better keep your eyes peeled!)
LISTEN! all around,
(can you hear any sound?)
If there's nothing that you
can see or can hear,
then hop right across –
you have nothing to fear!